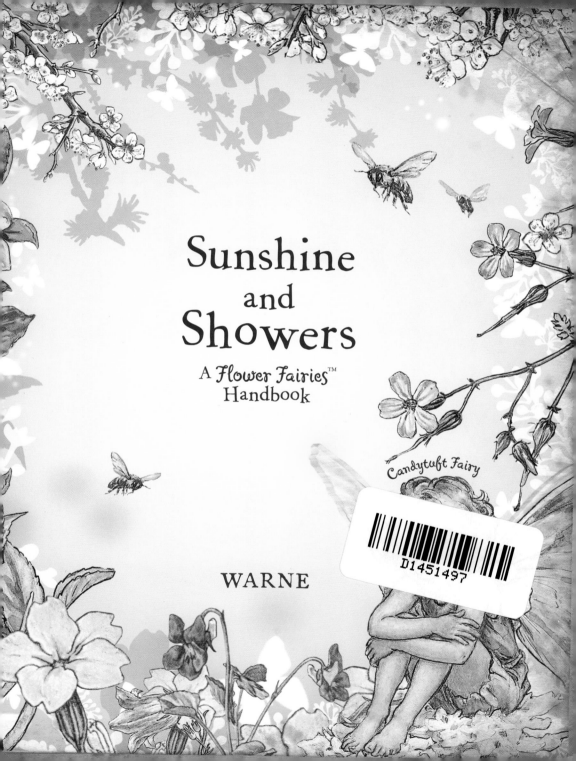

Sunshine and Showers

A *Flower Fairies*™ Handbook

Candytuft Fairy

WARNE

Cornflower Fairy

FREDERICK WARNE
Published by the Penguin Group
Penguin Books Ltd., 80 Strand,
London, WC2R ORL, England
Penguin Young Readers Group, 345 Hudson Street,
New York, New York 10014, U.S.A
Penguin Books Australia Ltd., 250 Camberwell Road,
Camberwell, Victoria 3124, Australia

1 3 5 7 9 10 8 6 4 2

Original poems written by Cicely Mary Barker, the creator of
the Flower Fairies, are credited to her with the initials CMB.

978-0-7232-6418-7

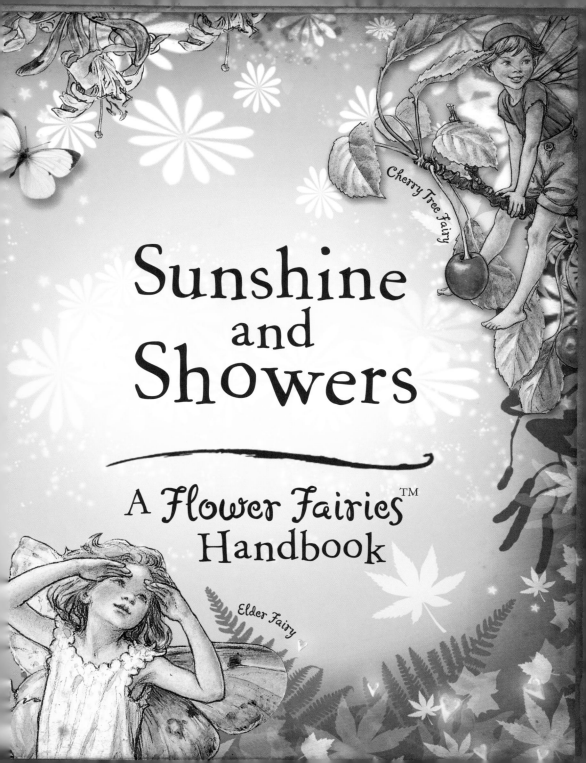

Sunshine and Showers

Cherry Tree Fairy

A *Flower Fairies*™ Handbook

Elder Fairy

Hello! I wonder who you are
and what you look like.
Are you a fairy like me?
I hope you will enjoy reading this little
book and find it useful.

I am leaving my comfortable corner of the garden
and setting off on a long journey. I'm going to live with
a Flower Fairy friend in a far off sunny place. I won't need
this handbook any more and would love you to have it.

The pages that follow offer hints and tips to guide you
through the year. I have carried it with me
every day, adding little notes here and there.
I am so pleased you are now the keeper of all
my special secrets!

Lots of love,
The Almond Blossom Fairy

This handbook belongs to:

Almond
Blossom

'rite your name here!

This is me!

Look inside...

Wild Cherry Blossom Fairy

Heliotrope

March

April

All Fool's Day

May

Spring Fling

Mothering Sunday

Easter

1
2
3
4
5
6
7
8
9
10
11
12
13
14
15
16
17
18
19
20
21
22
23
24
25
26
27
28
29
30
31

Spring

Tulip Fairy

Lilac Fairy

Wake up. It's Spring

Whether it's warm or wintery,
new life is springing up everywhere.

Birds and bees are beginning
to fly and buzz around and new
Flower Fairy babies are born.

Be a fairy friend:

Because so many babies are born in spring, there are lots of very busy fairy mothers! Always offer to help if you can.

Remember!

Be very careful where you step during the spring months. There are new tiny creatures all around you. Tripping over a baby bumble bee or a baby spider is not pleasant for anyone!

Forget-me-not Fairy baby

In hedgerows the blackthorn flowers into clouds of white blossom.

The garden comes alive and fairies bask in the warm sun.

In the woods, primroses and violets begin to push through the soil.

I've discovered:
This is a wonderful opportunity to flutter about and stretch your wings in the warm spring sunshine.

Blackthorn Fairy

Primrose Fairy

My Springtime Friends

Daffodil Fairy

"I'm the Daffodil Fairy
and my plant is the special flower for March.
You'll know that spring has arrived
when you see my bright yellow blooms!"

"I'm the Sweet Pea Fairy
the special flower for April.
All the fairy children love me because
I like to play. My little sister goes
everywhere with me. I teach her how to
keep our tendrils curly and how to train
our flowers to climb higher and higher.
We smell lovely too!"

Sweet Pea Fairies

Tip: Sweet Pea is a good fairy to know if you need a present for a baby. Her flowers make wonderful bonnets.

"I'm the Lily-
of-the-Valley Fairy,
the special flower for May.
When I begin to flower
all the fairies know that
warm weather and longer
days are on their way."

Lily-of-the-Valley Fairy

Note:

If you hear a tiny tinkling
sound early on a Spring
morning, it is probably just
the Lily-of-the-Valley Fairy
ringing her tiny bells and
trying to wake you up!

Tip:

Look out for bees and
wasps. They are friendly,
but big and noisy.

13

Tasks for Spring

This is the best time of year to clear the beds around your plant. Pull away last year's dead growth to make room for new shoots. These will need lots of space to stretch and grow.

Periwinkle Fairy

Tip: Carefully go through your clothes a shoes. Now is a good t for cleaning and m favorite things.

Be a fairy friend:

Ask around before you throw out old leaves and moss. Sometimes small animals who really feel the cold like to use it as extra bedding.

Greater Celandin Fairy

14

Pear Blossom Fairy

The Spring Fling is an important celebration for fairies everywhere (see page 19). You will need lots and lots of petals for costumes and decorations.

Pear, Almond and Wild Cherry Blossom Fairies will be happy to give you armfuls of pastel petals if you remember to ask in plenty of time.

Tansy Fairy

I've discovered:

The Tansy Fairy will help with your costume for the Spring Fling. Look for her out in the meadow. Appointments are not necessary.

Here I am again!

15

Notes and Sayings

Narcissus Fairy

March winds and April showers
Bring forth May flowers

Tip:
Narcissus gives young
fairies singing lessons
every spring. Find her
by the stream.

The World is very old;
But every Spring
It groweth young again,
And fairies sing.
CMB

Be a fairy friend:
Flower Fairy babies are born whenever
the seed of a new plant begins to grow.
If it's very windy and you see seeds
being blown far away from their plants
try to catch and return them.

Apple Blossom Fa...

Wash your face in dew on the morning of May 1 and you will have wonderful skin all year round!

The Fairy Queen can often be spotted at this time of year. Her correct title is Queen of the Meadow. Note that she doesn't wear a crown, but a necklace of pretty green berries.

I've discovered:
The Fairy Queen is very friendly and loves to chat to her fairy subjects. Remember it's polite to curtsey if you meet her.

Queen of the Meadow Fairy

Elder Rose Fairy

Special Events

April 1 is All Fool's Day, when it is traditional to play jokes and tricks on each other.

Mothering Sunday usually takes place in May. It is a special day when we show our mothers how much we love them.

Sycamore Fairy

Larch

Colt's-foot Fairy

Cowslip Fairy

Be a fairy friend:
Take fairy mothers on flying visits to the seaside, or prepare a woodland picnic. They will love you for it!

Remember:
Avoid the woods on All Fool's Day. Tree fairies fill acorn cups with water and balance them on branches. If you happen to be walking underneath, you may get soaked!

The Spring Fling

The annual Spring Fling takes place at the start of May. One lucky fairy is chosen to be the Spring Queen, crowned with flowers and given bouquets of May blossoms. After the official crowning there is a great party for everyone.

Note: It's polite to offer the newly-crowned Spring Queen a kiss if she passes.

You will spend the whole night on your feet at the Spring Fling. Make sure that you wear very comfortable dancing slippers, and have plenty to eat and drink so you don't run out of energy!

Columbine Fairy

Tip: When you arrive, head straight for the honey and violet meringues. They are so delicious and often run out!

Double Daisy Fairy

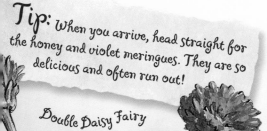

Tip: It's worth noting that early spring evenings can be very chilly. Order some large soft leaves from the Primrose Fairy to wear around your shoulders.

19

Poplar Fairy

Easter

The exact time of the Easter holiday changes every year, but it usually takes place in March or April.

Easter eggs – which symbolize new life – are traditionally given as gifts. Fairies generally exchange birds' eggs (once they have hatched of course!) filled with fruit, flowers or honey buns.

I've discovered: There is a lot of demand for fruits, nuts and buds to fill Easter eggs, so travel further away to fields and meadows to search. Make sure you pick up any empty eggshells you find well in advance so you have enough for all your friends and family!

Note: If you need to travel a long way, consider flying by bird. They offer good rates at this time of year. Try Air Cheep Cheep – comfy seats and nice snacks.

Treasure Hunts

There are often treasure hunts held for children at this time of year. The Crocus Fairies hide little goodies and treats all around the woodland glades under stones, in tree branches, behind toadstools, etc. Everybody enjoys these events and it is a good chance to get together as the weather becomes a little warmer.

These treasure hunts, and other ring games are usually held in the he Sunny Spot. You can find it by aveling eight flutters south of the Bluebell Fairy's home.

Note: If you are new to a particular area of Fairyopolis this is a great way for your fairy children to meet new friends.

Vetch Fairy

us Fairies

Cherry Tree Fairy

June

Vacation!

July

Sunset Ball

August

Magical Market

Traveller's Joy Fairy

Summer

Foxglove Fairy

Smile, it's Summer!

Summer is when most flowers are in bloom. It's a great time to visit other Flower Fairies and entertain friends, showing off your flowers at their best.

Every single petal
will be bursting with color!
Summer days are long, warm and sunny.
In fact sometimes August is too hot,
and flowers can get very thirsty.

Note: If August very hot, organize e alarm calls (ask a b butterfly to wake y they pass). Then f the lawn and gath cooling dew to k your blooms fre

Marigold Fairy

Geranium Fairy

In the hedges, all kinds of berries –
blackberries, hawthorn and sloe –
are beginning to ripen nicely.
These will provide food for
birds and other animals,
as well as for fairy feasts.

Mulberry Fairy

Remember:

There will be lots of insects around,
like grasshoppers, bees and ants.
They can be a little annoying, but
remember, mostly they are our friends.
So even though they can be noisy
and troublesome always try
to be polite.

My Summery Friends

"I'm the Wild Rose Fairy
and my plant is the special flower for June.
You'll often find me fluttering around
my blooms, picking off old petals
and choosing the softest ones
for my dresses."

Wild Rose Fairy

"I also make sweet perfumed
rosewater, which I give
to my fairy friends
whenever they visit."

Tip:
Pay a visit to the
Wild Rose Fairy.
Her perfume is
wonderful!

Poppy Fa

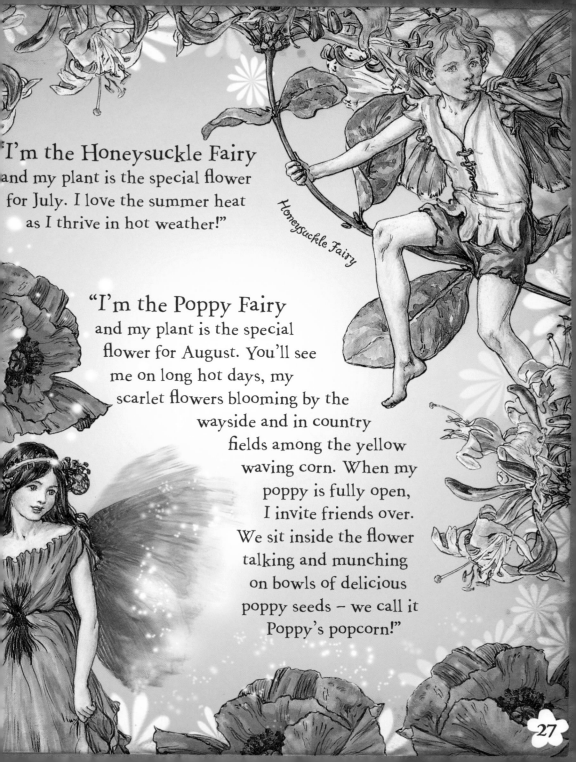

"I'm the Honeysuckle Fairy
and my plant is the special flower
for July. I love the summer heat
as I thrive in hot weather!"

Honeysuckle Fairy

"I'm the Poppy Fairy
and my plant is the special
flower for August. You'll see
me on long hot days, my
scarlet flowers blooming by the
wayside and in country
fields among the yellow
waving corn. When my
poppy is fully open,
I invite friends over.
We sit inside the flower
talking and munching
on bowls of delicious
poppy seeds – we call it
Poppy's popcorn!"

27

Things to Do

Search out the Strawberry Fairy.
Her delicious berries start off
green but will soon start to turn a rich red.
Take a couple to share with a friend somewhere
sunny and watch the sun go down.

Visit the wild Flower Fairies in the far
meadow. It's a bit of a walk to get there
– go to the pond and follow the path
behind the third tree until
you reach the buttercups.

Strawberry Fairy

Herb Robert Fairy

Be a fairy friend:

Fairy children love making daisy chains. Why don't you help them make some beautiful necklaces?

All fairies love an outdoor get-together. In the summer, a fairy picnic is just the thing.

Every fairy brings along something different to eat or drink and enjoys catching up with fairies visiting from far away.

It's nice to make the bees and butterflies feel welcome too because we don't really see much of them in any other season.

Daisy Fairy

Candytuft Fairy

Scabious Fairy

Thrift Fairy

29

Sunny Thoughts

Note: The sum doesn't start until the tree is in flower, so k an eye out!

Sometimes elves can be naughty, and try and find their way into parties without an invitation, disguised as fairies. There's a good way to catch them though. Pick buttercups and hold them under their chins. If you can't see the yellow color reflected on their faces, they're really elves!

Elder Fairy

Tip: When the sun gets too hot, stay in the shade beneath a big leaf.

Nasturtium Fairy

Magical Fact:
If you pick a rose on Midsummer's Eve it will still be fresh on Christmas Day! This only works if you're a fairy though!

Fairy folklore says that when June, July and August are very hot, January will be very cold. So be prepared!

Almost every clover plant has leaves divided into three smaller leaflets. If you happen to find one that has four, you will have good luck for the rest of the year!

Clover's Song

Little White Clover, kind and clean; Look at my threefold leaves so green!

CMB

White Clover Fairy

Special Events

The summer months are when fairies traditionally take their summer vacation. Make sure you tidy up well before you go, otherwise humans may notice your flower beds looking scruffy while you are away.

Tip:

Now is a good time to mak new warm bedding for wint Old-Man's Beard flowers a this time of year and produce lots of cozy fluff. Use this, an velvety pansy petals for stuffi mattresses, cushions and pillows

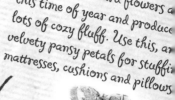

White Bindweed Fairy

Shirley Poppy Fairy

On the second Saturday of each
summer month fairies assemble
by moonlight for the magical market.
The weather is usually warm and the market
hillside hums with activity.
It's a great day out for the whole family.
Traders wear jingling bells on their clothes
and fly bright flags to entice customers
to buy their goods.

-Foot Trefoil Fairy

Mallow Fairy

Heather Fairy

Best Buys at
The Market:

- Bramble jam
- Baskets of berries
- Dandelion wine
- Fairy cakes
- Petal clothing

Sunset Ball

The Sunset Ball is held in July, and it's the biggest event of the fairy year. Every fairy, animal and insect in the garden gets dressed up and dances all night.

Organize your costume well in advance and order any extra petals, leaves and scent you may need. Everyone gets very busy during the days before the ball so be organized to avoid disappointment.

Nightshade Fairy

Lavender Fairy

Greater Knapweed Fairy

he Sunset Ball is always held on the lawn. With so
many fairies, all dancing together, the grass is often
n a bad state the next morning. Humans have often
oticed these strange circular patches of grass where
hundreds of tiny fairy feet have been trampling.
In fact they call them fairy rings!

I've discovered:

There are always tempting
violet bon bons, honey
drizzled roasted nuts and
tumblers of strawberry fizz at
the ball, so arrive early and
try everything!

Remember:

Make sure you are home
before dawn. However
much fun you are having,
it's not worth getting
caught.

Ragged
Robin
Fairy

September · October · November

The Autumn Market

Hallowe'en

Bonfire Night

Rose Hip Fairy

Privet Fairy

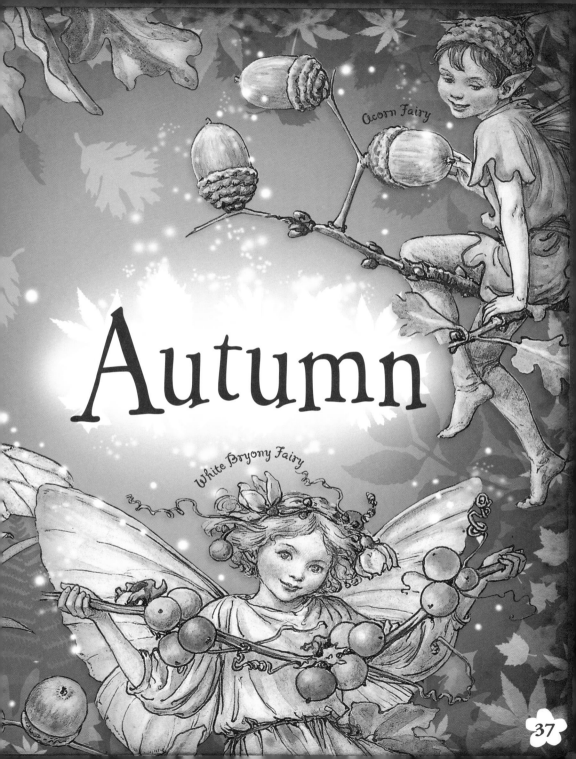

Acorn Fairy

Autumn

White Bryony Fairy

37

Horse Chestnut Fairy

Autumn Thoughts

In September summer begins to turn
into autumn, and lots of changes take place.
Leaves on trees turn yellow, orange and brown,
some animals begin storing food for hibernation and some
birds fly to sunnier places. The horse chestnut tree drops its
nuts to the ground in spiky green cases, and it's a good
time for berry picking.

Be a fairy friend:
Dormice and hedgehogs begin their
hibernation around this time so be
careful where you walk. Try to whisper
so as not to disturb dozing creatures.

Note: Towards the end
of autumn the skies are lit u
with noisy fireworks and wo
crackling bonfires. The nigh
are getting cold, the trees a
becoming barer and there
even be some frost.

As the days begin to turn chilly, some trees lose their leaves, and their bare branches give a wintery look to the landscape.

The hazelnuts ripen nicely. Any acorns that have not been eaten by the squirrels may start to grow into new oak trees.

The alder tree produces tiny cones and pretty catkins around this time of year.

Alder Fairy

Hazel-Nut Fairy

I've discovered:
Hazelnuts make a tasty snack throughout the year. Collect as many as you can in the autumn.

39

My Autumn Friends

"I'm the Nightshade Berry Fairy. I'm the special plant for September. My berries make wonderful glossy decorations but DO NOT eat them. They are poisonous! Make sure all fairy children are warned."

Nightshade Berry Fairy

Remember: Make sure all fairy children know what can be eaten and what will make them sick. Consult Self-Heal Fairy for further information.

"I'm the Michaelmas Daisy Fairy.
My plant is the special flower for October. When my white or blue flowers appear everyone knows that the cooler days of Winter are on their way. But it's still warm enough to play games of chase the butterflies."

Michaelmas Daisy Fairy

"I'm the Wayfaring Tree Fairy.
My tree is November's special plant. I stand on the side of the road, ready to greet tired travelers and make them smile. My fruits come in all colors and are a pretty sight for passers-by."

Note: Visit the Wayfaring Tree for pretty bags!

Wayfaring Tree Fairy

Magical Fact:
At night, the Michaelmas Daisy fairy sprinkles fairy dust into the yellow centers of her flowers. They become tiny lanterns and light up the woods, which is very useful now the evenings are getting darker.

Autumn Dangers

Tree fairies live high up in
the treetops. They spend
most of their time jumping and
swinging from branch to branch.
Beware – during autumn they just mess
about and giggle, often
falling onto fairy
passers-by. Remember
to look up!

Robin's Pincushion Fairy

42

We all love to watch the bright flames of bonfires and beautiful fireworks but always remember to keep a safe distance. Humans use bonfires to clear away dead leaves (which can help to keep our flowerbeds neat!) All fairies and creatures should take extra care in autumn because bonfires and fireworks are dangerous.

r Birch Fairy

Beechnut Fairy

Warning:
Be very careful. You could be quite happily playing in a pile of leaves, when, before you know it, you are surrounded by flames and you realize you are sitting on a bonfire!

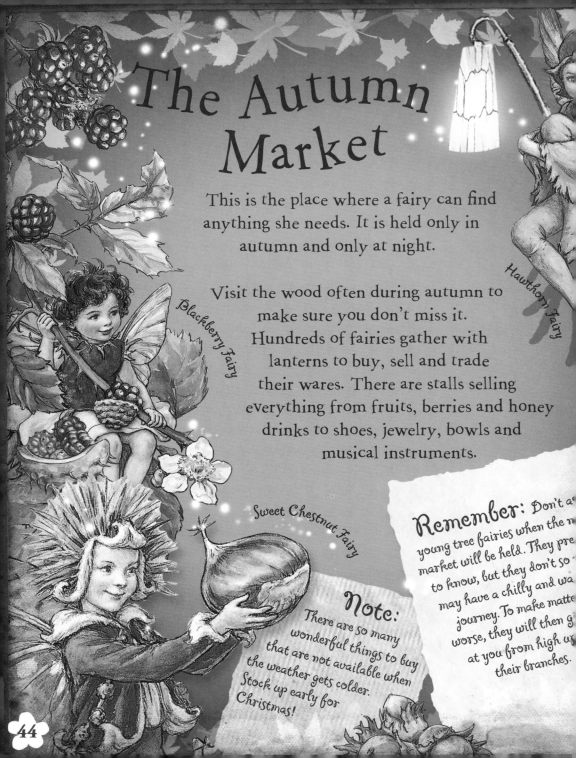

The Autumn Market

This is the place where a fairy can find anything she needs. It is held only in autumn and only at night.

Visit the wood often during autumn to make sure you don't miss it. Hundreds of fairies gather with lanterns to buy, sell and trade their wares. There are stalls selling everything from fruits, berries and honey drinks to shoes, jewelry, bowls and musical instruments.

Hawthorn Fairy

Blackberry Fairy

Sweet Chestnut Fairy

Remember: Don't a⸱
young tree fairies when the n
market will be held. They pre⸱
to know, but they don't so
may have a chilly and wa⸱
journey. To make matte⸱
worse, they will then g
at you from high u⸱
their branches.

Note:
There are so many wonderful things to buy that are not available when the weather gets colder. Stock up early for Christmas!

44

Fairy Gold

You will need special money for the autumn market. This takes the form of tiny seeds (dried), called Fairy Gold, that can be gathered from the center of your flowers. There are very many tempting things to buy at the market. Save up, by harvesting your seeds and storing them until you have enough for whatever you need to buy.

Mountain Ash Fairy

Magical Fact:
The fairy market will disappear instantly when the sun comes up. It's quite surprising the first time you see this happen. Don't wait too long to buy what you need.

45

Notes and Sayings

Fair on the first of September,
Fair for the month.

Note: This means if the weather is sunny and warm on the first of September, it will probably be nice all month!

You can often hear the Hazel-Nut
Fairy singing to children on
blowy autumn days.

I will tell the children
'You may take your share;
Come and fill your pockets,
But leave a few to spare.'
CMB

Gaillardia Fairy

Snapdragon Fairy

During the autumn months it is traditional to collect sloes from the Sloe Fairy. They are like plums but not so sweet. However, it's said that the sloes taste sweeter if they have been caught in an early frost.

Tip: Fairy children often use the different red and green berries of the Black Bryony Fairy as marbles. They make up great games together and keep busy on chilly autumn afternoons.

Black Bryony Fairy

Sloe Fairy

47

Elderberry Fairy

Hallowe'en

The Crab-apple Fairy

On the evening of October 31 all fairies celebrate Hallowe'en. It's a time to dress up and play tricks on each other. It's also traditionally a time for young fairies to visit friends and relatives to be given sweet treats.

Tip:
It's usually cold on the evening of Hallowe'en so wrap up well. Make a thick warm leaf, and colorful stockings part of your costume!

Note:
We love to play a game called apple bobbing. We put some crab-apples in a big bowl of water and then try to take bites without using our hands!

Bonfire Night

On November 5, fireworks
and bonfires are lit to celebrate
Bonfire Night.
(see page 43 regarding safety).

There are games to play and every
young fairy is allowed to stay up
late to enjoy cups of elderberry
wine and squares of chestnut
toffee. It's a wonderful time to
get together – midway between
summer and Christmas.

Dogwood Fairy

Tip:
he Hazel-Nut
airy and the
eechnut Fairy.
ey sell the most
delicious
roasted nuts.

Blackthorn Fairy

Pine Tree Fairy

December   January   February

A new year has begun

Valentine's Day

Christmas

50

Winter

Plane Tree Fairy

Burdock Fairy

A Winter Wonderland

Wintery days are short,
but can be crisp and bright.
Early morning frosts turn leaves
and grass silvery-white in the
woods and gardens.

Many trees are bare of leaves,
but look out for the first of the hazel
catkins – spring won't be far behind!

Note:

The seeds from Old-Man's Beard produce armfuls of silky fluff every winter. This can be hard to get hold of because the plants grow high up so gathering can be tricky. It's softer and longer lasting than dandelion fluff.

Old-Man's Beard Fairy

Tip:

Collect fluf
dandelion clo
when you see t
Use to fill wir
quilts and pille

Winter Jasmine Fairy

On the ground,
pretty snowdrops start to emerge,
and you may see a few dandelions
and other wild flowers.

As winter fades to spring,
color returns to the gardens
and hedgerows.
Look carefully to spy the
bright yellow flowers of
Winter Aconite.

Watch out!
Lots of the winter Flower
Fairies are boys.
They tend to
wake up early in
the mornings and
are very noisy!

I've discovered:
The Dandelion Fairy makes special
fluff-lined slippers. They are perfect for
keeping your feet warm during the cold
winter months.

Winter Aconite Fairy

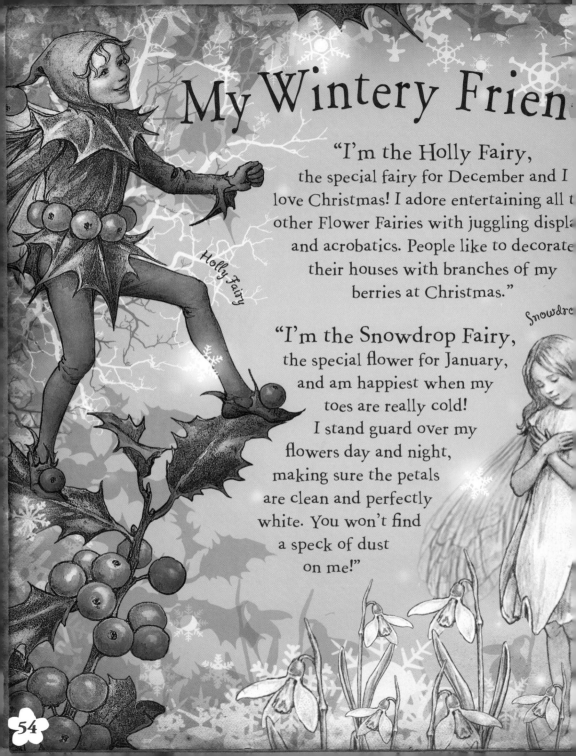

My Wintery Frien[d]

"I'm the Holly Fairy,
the special fairy for December and I
love Christmas! I adore entertaining all t[he]
other Flower Fairies with juggling displa[ys]
and acrobatics. People like to decorate
their houses with branches of my
berries at Christmas."

Holly Fairy

Snowdro[p]

"I'm the Snowdrop Fairy,
the special flower for January,
and am happiest when my
toes are really cold!
I stand guard over my
flowers day and night,
making sure the petals
are clean and perfectly
white. You won't find
a speck of dust
on me!"

"I'm the Iris Fairy, the special flower for February, and I live by the stream. You'll usually find me fluttering among the reeds and rushes, playing with the pond skaters and dragonflies. I am good friends with all the garden fairies and teach many of them to swim."

Iris Fairy

Remember:
These fairies don't feel the cold. If you are not a Winter Flower Fairy, make sure you always wear warm clothes and shoes.

Tip:
Look for Iris by the stream to ask about swimming lessons when the weather becomes warmer!

Notes and Sayings

"If in January the sun much appear March and April pay full dear!"

Some fairies say this means good weather in winter will lead to poor weather in spring.

It's important to make a note of the weather so you know what to expect for your flowers in a few months.

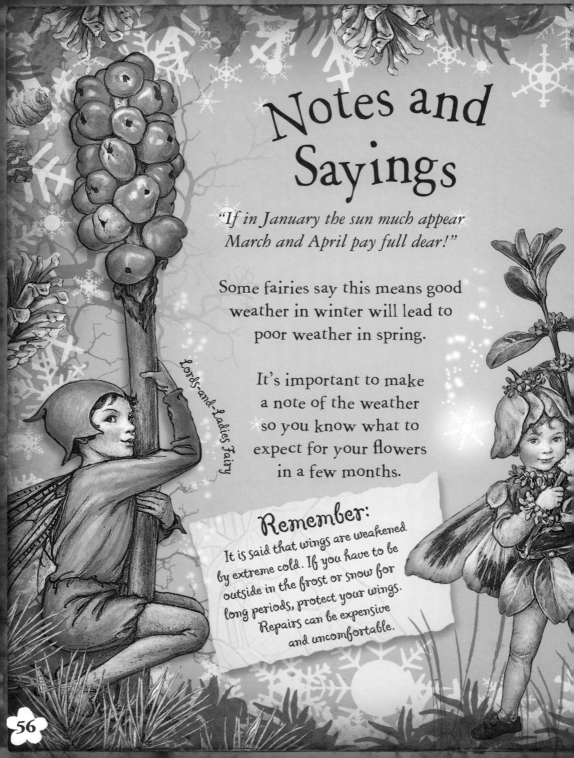

Lords-and-Ladies Fairy

Remember:

It is said that wings are weakened by extreme cold. If you have to be outside in the frost or snow for long periods, protect your wings. Repairs can be expensive and uncomfortable.

Beech Tree Fairy

Fairy rings are dark circles of grass that sometimes appear on the lawn (see page 35). If you see one, keep an eye out for humans. If a human steps into one they will be able to enter Fairyopolis, and they have really big feet (even the little ones!). Some of you can make yourselves invisible if you hear a human approaching, but not all.

Tip: Make sure fairy children around you know what their magical powers are. This will help them to stay safe and hidden when necessary.

x Tree Fairy

rb Robert Fairy

Jack-go-to-bed-at-noon Fairy

Christmas

A lot of the winter season is taken up
with preparations for Christmas.
It's a happy time when fairies get
together with friends and family.
They eat and sip delicious treats and
swap cards and presents.

Yew Fairy

Christmas

"I'm the Christmas Tree Fairy!
During the day I keep completely
still on top of the tree so that
no one notices me, but at night,
when everyone is asleep, I gently
step down and stretch my wings."

"I sometimes meet up with other
winter fairies for late night feasts.
We especially love small pieces of
mince pie and Christmas cake."

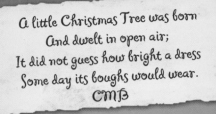

A little Christmas Tree was born
And dwelt in open air;
It did not guess how bright a dress
Some day its boughs would wear.
CMB

It's always nice to give and receive gifts, and Christmas is the most special time to do this. With honey from the bees, and fruit from the trees, you could make fragrant wines, sweet jams and delicious fairy jellies. Remember to collect thick dark green leaves to wrap gifts.

Remember:

Order lengths of grass for tying parcels in advance from Rush-Grass and Cotton-Grass fairies.
But remember, these two fairies are forgetful and always out and about having fun.
Confirm orders in advance or risk being disappointed.

Rush-Grass and Cotton-Grass Fairies

ll Fairies:

emember to take down
ur Christmas
ecorations by Twelfth
ight, or January 5.
's bad luck to leave
hem up any longer
han this.

59

Ragged Robin Fairy

New Year's Eve

On December 31,
we celebrate New Year's Eve.
There are parties everywhere and fairies
stay up late to welcome in the New Year.

At the stroke of midnight, throw petals at your
friends, sip warming cherry fizz and celebrate!

Horned Poppy Fairy

I've discovered:

After Christmas there are often little
scraps of glittery wrapping paper lying
around where humans have been. Use these
to wallpaper your home!

Remember:

It's worth noting that although fairy voices are very quiet, when lots of us are giggling and singing together, humans can hear us. Usually they think it's just far-away bells ringing in the New Year but be careful. The last thing we want is for them to start wandering about the garden at midnight. They might see us, or worse still, tread on us!

Hawthorn Fairy

All fairies should make a New Year's Resolution. This is a promise you make to yourself to change a bad habit or to try something new in the year ahead. Maybe it's to keep your flower bed or hedgerow tidier, or to help a neighboring fairy.

Valentine's Day

February 14 is Valentine's Day.
It's the best day of the year for
telling someone special how much
you love them.

Armfuls of rose blooms
make a perfect gift on
the day of love.

Rose Fairy

You don't have to give roses on Valentine's Day.
Here are some other flowers you could send,
and their very special meanings.

Pink carnation – I'll never forget you

Chrysanthemum – You're a wonderful friend

Sweet Pea – Thank you for a lovely time

White Camellia – You're adorable

Purple Hyacinth – Please forgive me

Yellow Lily – I'm walking on air

Gorse Fairies

I've discovered:
Visit the above Flower
Fairies yourself to obtain
the best rates, and hand
pick your blooms.

Notes About Your Birthday

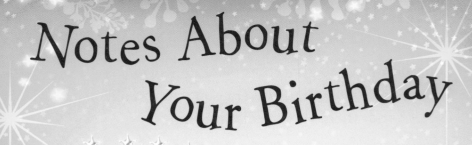

Pine Tree Fairy

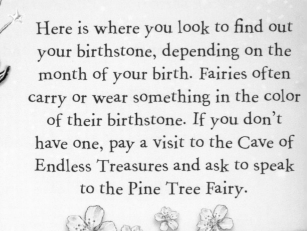

Here is where you look to find out your birthstone, depending on the month of your birth. Fairies often carry or wear something in the color of their birthstone. If you don't have one, pay a visit to the Cave of Endless Treasures and ask to speak to the Pine Tree Fairy.

Magical Fact:

All fairies believe that having a small birthstone and keeping it close to them, or wearing similar colors to their birthstone brings them good luck.

Spring Birthstones

March	April	May
	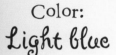	

Birthstone:
Aquamarine

Birthstone:
Diamond

Birthstone:
Emerald

Color:
Light blue

Color:
White

Color:
Bright green

...e fine dress of the pretty
...dy's-Smock Fairy is the
lightest of blues.

Look how white and pure
the Stitchwort Fairy's
blooms and dress are.

The tiny May Fairy always
wears her lucky birthstone
color, a clear bright green.

Summer Birthstones

June	July	August
Birthstone: **Pearl**	Birthstone: **Ruby**	Birthstone: **Peridot**
Color: **Cream**	Color: **Red**	Color: **Light green**
The cream color of White Clover's lovely flowers match her birthstone.	Cherry Tree keeps her birthstone close and always produces the juiciest fruits!	Green and cream colors suit Traveller's Joy perfectly.

Autumn Birthstones

September

Birthstone:
Sapphire

Color:
Deep blue

Bugle even carries a little bugle the same color as his birthstone!

October

Birthstone:
Opal

Color:
Rainbow!

Michaelmas daisies can be various shades from pale mauve to deep purple.

November

Birthstone:
Topaz

Color:
Yellow

Laburnum lights up the garden with her bright clothes and delicate blooms.

Winter Birthstones

December

Birthstone:
Turquoise

Color:
Sky blue

The Periwinkle Fairy's wings and blooms are the same blue as a cold but sunny winter day.

January

Birthstone:
Garnet

Color:
Dark red

Look at the dark red colors of the Yew Fairy's berries and clothes.

February

Birthstone:
Amethyst

Color:
Purple

Look at Dead-net delicate purple flo
He always wears pur

Horoscopes

Aries
Birthdays between March 21– April 20

Arians are natural leaders, being confident, adventurous, and enthusiastic. They have lots of energy and love new challenges.

Taurus
Birthdays between April 21– May 21

Taureans are good at getting things done as they are strong and determined. They are also patient, warm, loving, and generally nice to have around.

Gemini
Birthdays between May 22 - June 21

Geminis are always great fun as they are playful, lively, and creative. They love to learn and are very open to new ideas.

Cancer
Birthdays between June 22 - July 23

Fairies born under this sign are loving and protective and are usually very close to their families and flowers. They are also good listeners, being understanding and sympathetic.

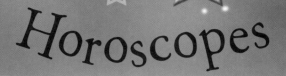

Horoscopes

Leo
Birthdays between July 24 – August 23
Leos are strong willed and determined and they always know exactly what they want. But they also make warm, loyal, and generous friends.

Virgo
Birthdays between August 24 – September 23
Fairies born under this sign are tidy and practical, and like everything in order. Though they can be shy at first, their natural charm makes them good company.

Libra
Birthdays between September 24 – October 23
Librans are gentle, easygoing fairies, who really appreciate beautiful things. They are great to have around, as they are sociable, fair, and kind.

Scorpio
Birthdays between October 24 – November 22
Scorpios are very exciting and determined fairies. Once they've made up their minds to do something there's no stopping them!

Dogwood Fairy

Horoscopes

Sagittarius

Birthdays between November 23 - December 21

Sagittarians are fun friends as they are usually outgoing, optimistic, and very honest. They are also quite adventurous and like traveling to new places.

Capricorn

Birthdays between December 22 - January 20

Capricorns are very loyal and have a great sense of humor. They are also hardworking, patient and reliable.

Aquarius

Birthdays between January 21 – February 19

Aquarians tend to be very creative and imaginative, so they often come up with great ideas. They are also known for being friendly and easygoing.

Pisces

Birthdays between February 20 – March 20

Pisceans are kind, gentle fairies who always like helping others. They are also very sensitive and understanding.

Snowdrop Fairy

For more fairy fun
with games and
activities visit
www.flowerfairies.com